THE ADVENTURES OF "CHUCK E. BEAVER" AND FRIENDS

FIRST DAY OF SCHOOL

Written by
Kiki

Illustrated by
ROBERT ELLIOTT

Published by
Montbec Inc.

Publisher
MATT ARENY

Publication Advisor
JOSE AZEVEDO

Editorial Supervisor
ETHEL SALTZMAN

Artwork Supervisor
PIERRE RENAUD

ISBN 2-89227-204-1

It was very early in the morning and the sun was just coming up.

This would be Chuck E.'s first day of school and he had been very nervous about it for some time .

Mr. and Mrs. Beaver were up now and were busy fixing breakfast.

"Chuck E.," yelled Mrs. Beaver, "are you up? Come on now! You don't want to be late for your first day of school, do you?"

Chuck E. was awake and had been most of the night. He had heard his mother and thought, "Late for school? I don't even want to go!"

"Why do I have to go to school?" thought Chuck E. "I can learn all there is to know right here at home."

"In fact I know enough already," Chuck E. said to himself. "I know how to tie my own shoes, brush my own teeth, and chop down trees just like my Pop!"

"How much more could I possibly learn that I don't know already?"

By now Chuck E. was just wasting time trying to put off having to go to school.

"Chuck E!" shouted Mrs. Beaver, "your breakfast is waiting for you, and if you don't hurry up you'll miss the school bus!"

"What's wrong with Chuck E. this morning?" wondered Mr. Beaver. "I thought he'd be looking forward to going to school just like all of his friends."

Mrs. Beaver smiled and replied, "Chuck E.'s just a little nervous and shy. After all it is his very first time being on his own without us."

"Just give him a little time. He'll get over it. When he sees all of his friends there, he won't feel so alone."

Chuck E. had just finished getting dressed and washing up. He thought he'd better come down for breakfast soon or Mom and Pop would be suspicious.

"Good morning, Pop, good morning, Mom." Chuck E. forced a smile as he entered the kitchen.

"Chuck E., what have you been doing upstairs all this time?" questioned Mr. Beaver. "You know this is a very important day and you don't want to be late, do you?"

"Of course not, Pop," replied Chuck E. "I was just taking a little more time so that I could look my absolute best."

"Well then, I guess that's okay," Mr. Beaver responded. "Nothing wrong with my boy looking good!"

Chuck E. heaved a big sigh of relief, knowing full well that his reasons for taking so much time were a bit different than what he had told his Pop.

"The school bus will be stopping at Chippy Chipmunk's house in five minutes," Mrs. Beaver said. "Chuck E., you can catch it there."

"Okay, Mom," said Chuck E. quietly.

"Chippy's house!" thought Chuck E. "I can find a good place to hide there for the day and Mom and Pop will never know that I didn't go to school."

Chuck E. felt much better with this in mind, knowing he wouldn't have to face so many strange people, especially his teacher.

Chuck E. finished his breakfast and kissed his Mom goodbye.

"Have a good day, Chuck E!" said Mrs. Beaver lovingly. "Don't worry, son, everything will be just fine at school."

"Of course it will be," Chuck E. thought to himself, "because I'm not going to be there."

Chuck E. left his house, with his lunch in his hand, on his way to Chippy's house.

On the road he came across his good friend Bobby Bear. "Hi, Bobby!" shouted Chuck E. "Where are you going so early in the morning?"

"Well, I'm supposed to be going to school for the first time," Bobby replied, "but I'd rather not."

"I know how you feel, Bobby," explained Chuck E. "I don't want to go either."

"I was thinking of hiding out at Chippy's house all day instead of going to that dumb old school!" Chuck E. looked at Bobby hopefully. "Say, Bobby, maybe you'd like to join me so I'll have someone to play with."

"That's a good idea, Chuck E!" replied Bobby. "Who needs school anyway?"

Now as Bobby and Chuck E.
approached Chippy's house they noticed
that many of their friends were there as
well. Gerty Goose, Marty Moose, and
Chippy Chipmunk were all anxiously
waiting for the school bus to arrive.

"Look, Bobby," shouted Chuck E.,
"There're all our friends!"

"Yeah!" replied Bobby. "Do you think
they're waiting for the school bus too?"

"They can't be," said Chuck E. "They look too happy and excited. How could anybody be happy about going to school?"

As Chuck E. and Bobby got closer to Chippy's house, Marty Moose suddenly noticed them. "Hey everyone, there's Chuck E. and Bobby!" shouted Marty. "This must be their first day at school!"

"Hi, Chuck E! Hi, Bobby!" everyone called. "You two must be really excited and looking forward to your first day at school," said Gerty.

"Well, to tell you the truth, Bobby and I don't really want to go," Chuck E. answered.

"Chuck E.'s right," agreed Bobby, "We won't know anyone, and who needs school anyway?"

"That's what we thought last year," Marty told them. "All of us were just as scared as you are, but you know something? We got through that first day and, in fact, we really enjoyed it!"

"Marty's right!" Chippy explained. "We found out that our teacher was very nice and we met many new friends that first day!"

"Do you think that might happen to us?" asked Bobby. "Do you think we could make new friends too?"

"Of course you can!" Marty replied. "Why, you'll have such a good time that you won't want to leave!"

"Do you really think so?" asked Chuck E. "I'm still afraid nobody will like me."

"Trust me, Chuck E.," Gerty assured him. "We went through this last year and we know everything will be just fine."

"I'll try, if Bobby will," Chuck E. said.

"Okay," Bobby agreed.

Just at that moment the school bus rounded the corner and stopped right in front of Chippy's house.

As the children were getting on the bus Chuck E. looked up and noticed that the driver was Mrs. Bear.

"Well, hello, Chuck E.," Mrs. Bear said. "Is this your first day at school?"

"Yes, Ma'am," Chuck E. replied.

"Well, don't you worry, you're going to have a wonderful time at school!" Mrs. Bear remarked.

"Thanks! I hope so," Chuck E. said without much conviction.

Chuck E. thought it was nice seeing a lot of familiar faces on his first day of school. It helped to make it a little less scary.

As the bus continued on its way to school it made a few more stops to pick up more children. Many of them Chuck E. didn't know, but he did notice that a lot of them seemed to be just as nervous as he was.

Chuck E. looked out the window and saw that they were very close to the school.

"Oh! Oh!" Chuck E. thought, "there's no turning back now!"

As the bus pulled to a stop in front of the school, all of the children jumped up and filed off the bus.

"Still looks pretty scary to me," Bobby exclaimed. "I don't know if we should go in there."

"Come on, Bobby!" Chuck E. replied. "You promised to stay with me."

At that moment the school bell rang loudly and all of the children hurried inside.

The last two to pass through the school doors were Chuck E. and Bobby.

As they walked down the hallway they came across a door marked "KINDERGARTEN" and they walked in slowly.

Inside they saw many desks with chairs arranged in rows. Chuck E. pointed out to Bobby the last two chairs that were empty at the front of the class.

"Oh, no!" thought Chuck E. "Not at the front of the class so everyone can see us!"

Just at that moment the teacher walked into the room and introduced herself.

"Hello, children! My name is Mrs. Groundhog and I am your teacher this year," she said.

"I am looking forward to getting to know each and every one of you."

"That's strange," Chuck E. thought. "I didn't expect my teacher to be so friendly."

"Now to begin with, students, I would like each person to turn around and say hello to the person behind them," Mrs. Groundhog continued. "I want us all to get to know one another and have fun together!"

Chuck E. felt extremely nervous about having to turn around and introduce himself to a stranger but he finally did, and to his surprise sitting right behind him was a little girl beaver.

"H-H-Hello, my name is Chuck E.," he said shaking.

"Hi, Chuck E., my name is Belinda," she said shyly. "It's very nice to meet you."

A big, shy smile came to Chuck E.'s face at that moment. "Yes, it-it is very nice to meet you, too," he replied.

Chuck E. turned around and felt very good that he had met a new friend like Belinda.

As the day continued Chuck E. learned many interesting things from painting to crayoning, to counting and learning how to read.

Chuck E. was having so much fun with his new friends that when the school bell rang to end the day he didn't want to leave.

As the other children were getting their coats on to leave for home, Chuck E. was still busy crayoning at his desk.

"Chuck E!" Mrs. Groundhog called. "Are you going to get ready to go home?"

"Do I have to, Mrs. Groundhog?" Chuck E. replied. "I'm having too much fun to go home now!"

"I'm afraid so, Chuck E.," Mrs. Groundhog explained. "but remember, you can come back tomorrow bright and early!"

"Oh, boy!" Chuck E. shouted, "I can't wait!"

Chuck E. jumped up and ran out the door. As he hurried to catch the school bus, he noticed Belinda walking by herself.

"Hello, Belinda!" Chuck E. beamed. "Can I sit with you on the school bus on the way home?"

"Yes, I'd really like that," Belinda answered.

Chuck E. smiled and thought to himself: "School is great! how could anyone feel scared about going?"

When Chuck E. arrived home he ran right to his room and jumped into bed. He wanted the next day to come quickly so he could go to school again.

Things don't always turn out as bad

As you think they might.

Put your best effort forward

And they usually turn out just right!

Your friend,

Chuck E.